D0822672

DISCARDED

Heartwall

Richard Jackson

University of Massachusetts Press   Amherst

Copyright © 2000 by
University of Massachusetts Press
All rights reserved
Printed in the United States of America
LC 00-024205
ISBN 1-55849-257-7

Designed by Sally Nichols
Set in Perpetua on a Macintosh G3
Printed and bound by Sheridan Books, Inc.

Library of Congress Cataloging-in Publication Data
    Jackson, Richard, 1946–
        Heartwall / Richard Jackson.
            p. cm.
        ISBN 1-55849-257-7 (paper : alk. paper)
            I. Title.
    PS3560.A242 H4 2000   00-024205
    811'.54—dc21

British Library Cataloguing in Publication data are available

Growth.
Heartwall by heartwall
adds on petals.

One more word like this, and the hammers
will be swinging free.

> Paul Celan

Methought she purged the air of pestilence,
That instant was I turned into a hart,
And my desires, like fell and cruel hounds,
E'er since pursue me.

> *Twelfth Night* 1.1.21$\frac{1}{N}$24

Any wound rather than a wound of the heart.

> *Ecclesiastes* 25:13

for Terri, for Amy
&
in memory of Bill

Contents

Acknowledgments

I would like to thank the Faculty Research Committee at the University of Tennessee, Chattanooga, for its support.

Anthologies:
Best American Poems 1997 (New York: Scribners, 1997)
      Poem Once Called Desperate . . .
Homewords (Knoxville: University of Tennessee Press, 1996)
      Do Not Duplicate This Key
Introspections (Hanover, N.H.: University Press of New England, 1997)
      Do Not Duplicate This Key
Literature (Upper Saddle River, N.J.: Prentice Hall, 1996)
      Benediction (earlier version)
New Bread Loaf Anthology (Hanover, N.H.: University Press of New England, 1999)
      Reincarnation of a Lovebird
      Filling in the Graves
Orpheus & Company (Hanover, N.H.: University Press of New England, 1999)
      Antigone Today
Pushcart Prize Poems XX (Wainscott, N.Y.: Pushcart Press, 1996)
      Basic Algebra
Pushcart Prize Poems XXI (Wainscott, N.Y.: Pushcart Press, 1997)
      No Turn on Red

Magazines:
Atlanta Review
      You Can't Get the Facts Until . . . (1995)
      Basic Algebra (1995)
      Decaf Zombies of the Heart (2000)
      The Sentimental Poem I Almost Didn't Write (1998)
Black Warrior Review
      Waiting For Kafka (1993)
Bloomsbury Review
      Heartless Poem (1995)
Crab Orchard Review
      No Man's Land (1996)
      Grammar Rules (1996)
Crazyhorse
      My Black Madonna (1992)
Georgia Review
      Objects in this Mirror . . . (2000)
Gettysburg Review
      Buy One, Get One Free (1995)

Harvard Poetry Review
>New and Selected Posthumous Poems (2000)
>Things I Forgot To Put . . . (1997)

Marlboro Review
>No Turn on Red (1996)
>Antigone Today (1998)

Maryland Poetry Review
>Sonata of Love's History (1997)

Mid-American Review
>Benediction (2000)
>No Fault Love (1998)

New England Review
>Unauthorized Autobiography (1993)

North American Review
>Poem Once Called Desperate . . . (1996)

Prairie Schooner
>Benediction (earlier version) (1993)
>Liberation Theology (1999)

Tar River Review
>Terzanelle of Kosovo Fields (2000)

Third Coast
>Do Not Duplicate This Key (1996)
>Job's Epilogue (1998)
>Reincarnation of a Lovebird (1998)

Translated Versions:

Helicon 1999 (Israel)
>Possibility

Literatura 1999 (Slovenia)
>Antigone Today
>Poem Once Called Desperate . . .
>Possibility
>Reincarnation of a Lovebird
>Objects in this Mirror . . .

Nova Revija (Slovenia)
>Possibility

PEN 96 (UK/Slovenia)
>Antigone Today

Vilenica 95 (Slovenia)
>You Can't Get the Facts

Vilenica 99 (Slovenia)
>Possibility
>Reincarnation of a Lovebird

Heartwall

I

Soon the great city was all monsters, high bred
& parti-coloured comfy, digging in
like a really bad dream.

Now rules were promulgated at the City Centre.
Those with more eyes, cast ruthlessly aside,
lurked to the suburbs.
The airport was closed down. Animals were untied.
Thought of his kind ground & lurched to a halt,
all nouns became verbs.

Was all this the result of a failure of love,
he hailed a passing stranger, a young girl
with several legs.

        Berryman, Dream Song #368

Antigone Today

It turns out the whole sky is a wall.
It turns out we all drink from history's footprints.
One day the stones seemed to open like flowers
and I walked over the orphaned ground for my brother.
Even now I can count every barb in the wire.
The stars were covered with sand.
The sandstorm had almost covered the body.
I dug around him, covered him myself.
Today, each memory is a cemetery that must be
tended. You have to stand clear of the briars of anger.
You have to wash revenge from your eyes.
Sophocles kept seeing me as a bird
whose nest is robbed, screeching hysterically.
In another place a flock of birds tear themselves apart
to warn the king of what will happen to his state.
I don't know who I am. I hardly said a word.
I think Sophocles knew what I might mean,
and was afraid. Everything I did was under
one swoop of the owl's wing. Who is anything
in that time? And he never listened.
Even the sentry's words dropped their meanings
and fumbled like schoolboys forgetting their lessons.
What I dug up was a new word for justice,
a whole new dictionary for love. But why did my own
love desert me? He came too late. He was
another foolish gesture from another age. What I tried
to cover with dust was the past, was anger, was revenge.
Now you can see it all in mass graves everywhere.
You can see it in the torture chambers,
the broken mosques and churches, the sniper scopes.
You can see it in the women raped by the thousand.
Who is any one of us in all that?
Who was I? I've become someone's idea of me.
You can no longer read the wax seal of the sun.
The trees no longer mention anything about the wind.
I don't see who could play me later on.
It turns out I am buried myself.
It turns out we are all buried alive
in the chamber of someone else's heart.

Objects in This Mirror Are Closer Than They Appear

Because the dawn empties its pockets of our nightmares.
Because the wings of birds are dusty with fear.
      Because another war has eaten its way
      into the granary of stars. What can console us?

Is there so little left to love? Is belief just the poacher's
searchlight that always blinds us, and memory just
      the tracer rounds of desire? Last night,
      under the broken rudder of the moon, soldiers

cut a girl's finger off for the ring, then shot her and the boy
who tried to hide under a cloak of woods beyond their Kosovo
      town. Listen to me,—we have become words
      without meanings, rituals learned from dried

riverbeds and the cellars of fire-bombed houses.
Excuses flutter their wings. Another mortar round is
      arriving from the hills. How long would you say
      it takes despair to file down a heart?

When, this morning, you woke beside me, you were mumbling
how yesterday our words seemed to brush over the marsh
      grass the way those herons planed over
      a morning of ground birds panicking in their nests.

When my father left me his GI compass, telling me
it was to keep me from losing myself, I never thought
      where it had led him, or would lead me. Today,
      beside you, I remembered simply the way you eat

a persimmon, and thought it would be impossible for each
drop of rain not to want to touch you. Maybe the names
      of these simple objects, returning this morning
      like falcons, will console us. Maybe we can love

not just within the darkness, but because of it. Ours is
the dream of the snail hoping to leave its track on the moon.
      We are sending signals to worlds more distant
      than what the radio astronomers can listen for, and yet—

And yet, what? Maybe your seeds of daylight will take root.
Maybe it is for you the sea lifts its shoulders to the moon,
          for you the smoke of some battle takes the shape of a tree.
          On your balconies of desire, in your alleyways of touch,

each object is a door opening like the luminous face of
a pocket watch. Maybe because of you the stars, too,
          desire one another across their infinite,
          impossible distances forever, so that it is not

unthinkable that some bird skims the narrow sky where
the sentry fires have dampened, where the soldier, stacking
          guns in Death's courtyard, might look up, and remember
          touching some story he carries in his pockets, a morning

like this blazing through the keyholes of history, seeing not
his enemy but those lovers, reaching for each other, reaching
          toward any of us, their words splintering on the sky,
          the gloves of their hearts looking for anyone's hands.

Do Not Duplicate This Key

It is not commonly understood why my love is so deadly.
At the very least it uproots the trees of your heart.
It interferes with the navigation of airplanes like certain
electronic devices. It leaves a bruise in the shape of a rose.
It kisses the dreamless foreheads of stones.
Sometimes the light is wounded by my dark cliffs.
Around me even the moon must be kept on a leash.
Whenever I turn you will turn like a flower following
the day's light. Sometimes I feel like Ovid's Jove,
hiding behind the clouds and hills, waiting for you
to happen along some pastoral dell thinking
what I might turn you into next. Then I remember
the way he turned himself into a drooling bull to scour
the pastures of Arcadia for Europa. Forget myth, then.
Forget Ovid. According to Paracelsus, God left the world
unfinished from a lack of professional interest
and only my love can complete or destroy it.
Sometimes I come home, open a bottle of Chalone
Pinot Blanc and listen to the Spin Doctors'
"How Could You Want Him (When You Could Have Me)?"
My love is so deadly because it holds a gun to every despair.
But this is not the case everywhere. In some places
the heart's shrapnel shreds our only dreams. Even
the trees refuse to believe in one another. Sometimes
it seems we've put a sheet over Love and tagged its toe.
Someone thinks it lives in the mother of the Azeri soldier,
Elkhan Husseinar, because she puts, in a jar on his grave,
the pickled heart of an enemy Armenian soldier.
This is love, she says, *this is devotion*.
Someone else assigns Love a curfew. There's the 25-year-old
sniper who targets women in Sarajevo to see
what he calls "their fantastic faces of love"
as they glance toward their scrambling children.
This is when the seeds desert their furrows for rock.
This is when Despair pulls a Saturday Night Special
from its pocket and points it at the cashier in the 7–11 store.
This is when it seems each star is just a chink in our dungeon.
It is at this hour that I think entirely about you.
My love is so deadly because it wants to handcuff

the Death that has put all our lives on parole.
I myself escaped long ago from Love's orphanage.
I invented a world where the moon tips its hat at me.
I have this way of inventing our love by letting
my words rest like a hand on your thigh.
I have this way of gently biting your nipples
just to feel your body curl like the petal of a rose.
Even when I sleep you can detect my love
with the same instruments scientists use to see
the microwave afterglow of the Big Bang that created
the universe. My love is so deadly
the whole world is reinvented just as Paracelsus said.
I love even the 90 percent of the universe that is dark matter
no light will ever embrace. Rilke died from the thorn
of a rose because he thought his love was not so deadly.
My love is so deadly it picks the blossoming fruit tree
of the entire night sky. I can feel, in the deepest part
of you, the soft petals stir and fold with the dusk.
So deadly is my love
the call of the owl is thankful
to find a home in my ear. The smoke
from my cigarette thanks me for releasing it.
The tree changes into a flock of birds.
So deadly is my love other loves fall asleep in its throat.
It is a window not attached to any wall.
It is a boat whose sails are made of days and hours.
It rises like Botticelli's Venus from the sea.
This is not some idle myth.
In fact, it has been discovered that all life
probably began on the surface of deep sea bubbles
which came together in Nature's little cocktail party
carrying most of the weird little elements we are made of,
the kind of molecular sex that excites chemists.
My love is so deadly it starts spontaneous combustions.
The whole universe grows frightened for what comes next.
The sky undresses into dawn, then shyly covers its stars.
Sometimes I think your love is a compass pointing away.
Sometimes I discover my love like the little chunks of moon
they dig from under the Antarctic ice. My love is
so deadly it will outlast Thomas Edison's last breath
which has been kept alive in a test tube

in Henry Ford's village, Dearborn, Michigan. Even the skeptic,
David Hume, 1711–1776, begins to believe in my love.
My own steps have long since abandoned their tracks.
My own love is not a key that can be duplicated.
It knocks at the door of the speakeasy in Sarajevo
and whispers the right word to a girl named Tatayana.
This, of course, was from before the war,
before everybody's hearts had been amputated from their lives.
Now my love abandons all my theories for it.
This is why my love seems so deadly.
It is scraping its feet on your doormat, about to enter.
Sometimes you have to cut your life down
out of the tree it has been hanging in. My love is
so deadly because it knows the snake that curls inside
each star like one of Van Gogh's brush strokes.
My love is so deadly because it knows the desire of the rain
for the earth, how the astronomer feels watching
the sleeping galaxies drift away from us each night.
I am listening to your own rainy voice.
I am watching the heart's barometer rise and fall.
I am watching like the spider from your easel.
My love is so deadly, birds abandon the sluggish air.
Their hearts fall from trees like last year's nests.
The smoke awakens in the fire. The rose abandons the trellis.
My love is so deadly it picks the locks of your words.
And even tonight, while someone else's love tries
to scavenge a few feelings from a dumpster, while someone
lies across the exhaust grating like a spent lover,
my own love steps out from my favorite bar under
a sky full of thorns, weaving
a little down the sidewalk, daring the cabs
and after hours kamikazes like someone stumbling
back into a world redeemed by
the heart's pawn tickets, holding a pair of shoes
in one hand, a hope that breathes in the other.

Reincarnation of a Lovebird

What's wrong with money is what's wrong with love;
it spurns those who need it most for someone
already rolling in it.

William Matthews

Already it is snowing, the branches spattering out of darkness
the way I imagine the nerve endings of that grasshopper
did on my sill last summer while the nightingale finished it.
Already old fears condense on the panes with you
a thousand miles or words away, my friend
recently buried, the light in my room blaring all night
the way it's done in prisons, trying to keep too much emotion
from scurrying out of the corners. There's a blind spot in
the middle of your eye, the guilt you feel for loving so fully
in the face of death, or dying in spite of love's power.
These verbs are searchlights for memories gone over the wall.
It's all we can do to embrace the distance between us
while night limps across these rooftops, while we preside
over the heart's fire sale. Outside the streetlights hook
a reluctant sky. Memory won't save everything.
That nightingale disappeared into the piracantha bush
to flute a melody we call imitation but may only be
another lie. Charlie Mingus's bass would die
into an arrangement, then reincarnate itself as a form of
love. It's time to decide if this is an elegy or a love
poem lurking behind one of the smoked glass windshields
that go up or down the street every few minutes. What we
should have said to each other waits like an insect
all winter for a false spring. The language of stars
no longer brings consolation or love. The Egyptians
invented the phrase, "eat, drink, and be merry,"
you know the rest, but kept a skeleton
hung at dinner parties in case you tried to forget.
My love, the heart taps its way along sidewalks
like a blind man and muggers are gleeful on the corners.
What we need are more emergency vehicles for the soul.
We need to knock at the door of the heart's timekeeper.
The tracks I'll leave later when I go out into the purity
of snow will destroy it. The scientist's light
on the atom alters what should be there.
Every glass we raise we eventually have to lower.

Possibility

Occasionally, the wind stumbles, kicks at the dirt,
until a fossil tries to lift its head toward the moon,
two old bones, two stories that call to the huntsman's
hounds. Upon which a vagrant light pauses
like an insect, upon which the archeologist's sight
never falls. And the whole landscape seems littered
with fallen dreams. Sycamores too, threading
the air, dropping pods of seed, tiny skulls
holding imagined shapes that will never appear.
Occasionally, you can hear starlight tapping
on your window. Occasionally, you can hear
the whispers of mollusks, the air in the hawk's wing.
How is it possible to describe any of this?
Fish dream of a moon that rests on the water
like a lily pad, and that moment is enough.
The stream tries to forget the silence of its beginnings.
The cowbird lays its eggs in other nests so
that the offspring become something totally other.
Our souls waver in the grass and only record
the damp impressions of some sleeping animal.
The early buds shrivel with frost.
Suddenly it seems memory is impossible.
Who can say what fills the coffin of the moment?
Are we, then, like moths at a candle, glowing
longer than life is left in us? I don't know
how much longer it is possible to stay in a poem
like this one, sifting through the ashes of
the future.

             I was saying this when you arrived
over the sound of the woodpecker on the tree
outside my window where each morning I watch
the day climb into the branches, where
each morning at 3 A.M. for a few hours I hear
the mockingbird trying to become anyone else, and so
you arrive, then, desire walking behind you like an empty
pair of shoes. Far off, a radio telescope
crackles with news from all directions of the cosmos
from a time when we handled stars as carefully
as precious stones. And this, too, tells us there is

not enough mass to keep us all from eventually flying
apart. All this, too, abandons us. Not deliberately
the way frogs and crickets quiet their whole
being at our approach. But as their nature
demands. The dogwood will blossom open
white, angelic, but not necessarily for us who remember
it is also a tree of crucifixions, of one man abandoned.
Is there any way to translate all this into joy?

Whose hands, after all, have not, at some time,
been singed by a star? How can we understand
that time exists only *between* moments?
Maybe it is enough that we blindfold all our words.
There is so much, perhaps, we want to bury
beneath the wind. How we locked our own prayers
in dungeons. How we strangled someone's love
in the alleyways of our own despair. How we abandoned
whole planets like principles. Our own sins are
more grievous than the deaths of stars.
Our house is Time but it is leaking
our last chances. Each breath is a map of our desires.
Each map a blank page. We would have to wait
for the stones to waken to make amends.
Each star guards a secret. Each secret is a hive
of regrets. The past is smoldering, still.
It is not memory we want, but forgiveness.
We rub our hands against the dusk.
Out of which sunsets blossom.
Out of which the fossil reappears as the moon.
Out of which your footsteps weigh, but lightly,
on my soul, you, for whom relation
darts wildly about like a bat in the rafters,
gathering the last scraps of daylight held in
abandoned mirrors, you, hoisting the heaviness
of each failed dream, for it is you I touch as we shift
the burden of our desires from one shoulder to another,
as we watch the swallow's flight decipher the landscape,
as the scarecrows of feeling are trying on our words,
for who can say, now, how many stars are missing?

Waiting for Kafka

I turn on the light. The wind
digs its spurs into the trees.
I watch the rain. The dog comes in
out of the rain and shakes off the past.
I grind some coffee. The owls rasp.
Beneath me the continent continues to shift
toward a time when all the land on earth
will mass together again then start to separate
for another five hundred million years. Meanwhile,
I watch the old dreams sitting around lethargically
like the whores in a painting by Toulouse-Lautrec.
He must have understood why
there is no concept in physics of a temperature
for single bodies. Loneliness is trying
to force the rear windows. I open
the refrigerator to check on the oplatky,
Kafka's favorite pastry. I set aside
some cognac. The first birds are carrying off
little bits of night in their beaks.
A few others hover overhead
like unfinished dreams. I sip some coffee.
I read the paper. I light a cigarette.

Just about now Franz must be stepping out
the door of his cramped little house
on castle hill. Around the corner they used
to post the plague bills. In 1720 the brown rat
whose fleas stay with their host to nest
supplanted the black rat whose fleas migrate
and thus effectively put an end to the plague.
Today we do a better job than any disease.
Now there is news of a brief cease-fire
in Sarajevo. Maybe it will be so calm
the stars will sleepwalk across the sky.
The souls of ancient birds will sing in their trees.

I punch in a tape of Kafka's favorite
Mendelssohn. I can hear the early morning
truck picking up what's left of our lives
at the curbing. I open the blinds. I feed the dog.
Young Franz pauses at his threshold.
He will not even sleep with Dora or any woman

12

until the last year of his life, trapped
at his home until he is thirty. No wonder
his speakers are worms and insects.
For now, all the old hurts have dropped anchor.
His past month has been just a slamming of doors
on whatever Hope came begging and crippled.
He is finishing one of his stories
he will later try to burn. In one, an ape
lectures the academy. He is making fun
of Newton's neat little world. It is one hundred years
too early for Kafka to know it is probably
mites that transfer genetic information
from one species to another during evolution.
Who will ever open the back door
of his heart? There's a storm breaking out
deep inside his mirror. I may be waiting all day.
I slice an onion for soup. I set the table.
There is much to discuss. The trees
have been trying to follow their shadows
across the road. And today I discovered
the heart is an onion. You can see
the whole thing in cross section
like one of those medieval pictures
of the cosmos all the way from the outer ether
to the little picture of a spread-eagled man.
Each of our lives hangs tenuously
to one of those brown flakes that cover
the yellow core. Why is this so unbelievable?

Yesterday I found out the soul is a broken
telephone booth. I'll tell you what makes
no sense: since yesterday was a multiple of nine
the superstitious generals in what used to be
Burma knew it must be safe to slaughter
the rebel villagers again. Just as I did once,
at Monsanto Chemical Company, someone will turn
a valve because there is a shift in the wind.
We are all living in our little prisons of light.
I turn off the light. I put the soup on simmer.
This morning as I woke a robin fell from a branch
like a carnival target. And just last night I saw
a worm eating its way through Newton's apple.

Filling in the Graves at a Cherokee Site

for John Anderson

Night walks through our days and no one notices.
We like to think of the intricate beauty of a swallow's flight,
but it is only a desperate, open-mouthed search for insects.
There are three truths you have taught me here: that
our shadows will desert us for other, better objects;
that Time steps away from the clock like the song of a blind bird;
and that our maps are the empty husks of desire. So, what can
we say, then, to the greed of men that has given us
these broken pieces of sky? You might as well try
to shake the wind until it crumbles. You can
almost scrape yourself on the nails of light hammered
through the trees where some stupid men have peeled
back the eyelids of the graves, their mocking words
strewn about like the rusted cans that flake in my hands.
Each of their thousand bottles left here is filled with dark.

You have this way of taking the smoke from the sage,
cupping it into your heart and smudging the whole
universe that gathers around you. Standing among all these
open eyes, I am afraid I will dissolve like the prey
the falcon leans toward. I am here with a woman for whom
even the stars shiver and I can tell you the light around her
tastes so sweet I could believe in your world that flies
above this one. I don't know how many of my words for her
have been siphoned into these lives. We are stepping
over the mussel shells of history.

                    Now the blue
herons are trying to gather the souls that hover
just above the water. Their calls fall around us
like a blanket. And who here is not buried in another
person's heart? Everything we breathe is a gift
from the past. This late in the season even the spider
webs have disappeared. A few stars are setting
into nests below the horizon. A few words like these are
never going to shovel the terrible past into place.
We can smell the overwhelming must of these graves,
the broken wings of these souls, but we will never smell

what they dreamt. Maybe it is all right. We are filling
our lives with whatever love they've left.

       Now the trees are going
to let their dreams fly out like bats, like herons,
like bees, like anything that lives and dies, the vapor
trail caught for a moment in the light before it disappears,
the moon starting to open its eyes with something like hope.

Unauthorized Autobiography

I want to be able to walk
into a party one night the way Giovanni Bernadone
did in the late thirteenth century
and wake from a trance the next morning
as St. Francis of Assisi talking with birds
about the secrets of astrocosmology.
According to the new cosmology we are
living in one of a billion parallel universes
originating from the big bang so that any
one of our stories includes invisible others
we can't even begin to count. Archimedes wanted
a method to count all the grains of sand
but ended up insulting a Roman legionnaire.
He didn't care if Archimedes was Archimedes.
He killed him. It was only natural,
given the way history can't lift its head
at the end of the bar, the way night has
turned out its pockets of knives instead of stars.

Out beside the road another war is stretching
and waking from its siesta beneath a tree
like one of Breughel's drunken farmers.

I want to be able to sit once again in David's Bar
and talk with my favorite angel, Gabriel,
about the meaning of the natural, just as William Blake
sat down to supper with Isaiah and Ezekiel
while writing his *Marriage of Heaven and Hell*.
In New Harmony, Indiana, Gabriel's footsteps are
fenced in behind a small church. In the eighteenth century,
Linnaeus wanted to create a zoo in Stockholm
to parallel the Eden he thought had never changed.
In the Eden of America everything evolves.
You can see the great American jackalope displayed
in Dubois, Wyoming, an animal with the speed
of an antelope and the body of a rabbit.
At Wall Drug in South Dakota you can see the mutant
flying jackalope. You can find fur-bearing trout
all over the Midwest. You can see

the concrete Eden in Lucas, Kansas, 113 tons
sculpted by Samuel Dinsmoor, the retired
Union soldier who preserved himself in a glass coffin.
In the Eden of America it is only natural to live forever.

In the Eden of Greece poor Persephone was picking
daffodils when moonlight slipped off her shoulders
like a shawl, catching the eye of Hades who grabbed her.
Now she spends her time divided between Paradise
and Hell. It was her mother, Demeter, who nearly
wiped out all the men on earth. It was my friend,
Jim Cryan, who took the pictures of what our
Agent Orange did in Vietnam. For years afterward
he would look at the recon photos until he started living
under his kitchen table. Now, he too spends his life
between Paradise and Hell. This is why
every hour wants to turn into a daffodil.
This is why the moon tries to hide her face each month.
It is only natural that we try to roll back the horizon
like a worn rug, only natural that laughter
casts dice for a few moments of joy.

Outside Sarajevo, a dozen soldiers seem to be playing
soccer with the moon. But it is not the moon.
It is the head of a Muslim boy blown apart
by a 155-millimeter howitzer shell. Only natural.
It is only natural that history's eyelids are drooping
at such a late hour. Truth is quivering
in the shadows, leaning against the door frame
of a bombed out house like a broken puppet,
waiting for her name to be drawn from a hat.
She is listening to the boy's mother invent
a story that is her garden of stars.
She is trying to remember the names sounded
in bell towers, the forests of old graves.

It is your name I am remembering now.
Since you left I have been living in the heart's
minefield. The moon has become a cocoon
of things we haven't yet dreamt.

My own story is caught among these others
like a bird in a thornbush. Maybe the fact
that our sun is one of only 15 percent without a companion star
helps to explain our loneliness. Even asteroids
naturally travel in pairs. You can see a double crater
near Hudson's Bay. On the other hand, there are
Black Widow Pulsars that come in pairs,
one cannibalizing the other for parts
like a used car salesman. Lately, I've been besieged
by their phone calls. Lately, too, I've been confused
by calls for lifetime guaranteed aluminum siding
and prepaid grave plots. In 1954 I first prepared for death
until the doctor showed me my tonsils
floating in a jar like cherries,
a fruit I've had difficulty eating ever since.

How much can they take away and leave anything
that is still us? Haydn, for instance, was buried eleven
years before they removed the body to Eisenstadt
and discovered the head was missing. Is that natural?
It was 150 years before someone returned the skull.
Haydn spent his life trying to find a pure, a single love,
and failed.
                        I want to watch each night
as you fold yourself into the daffodil. I want to be there
each morning at low tide as the lovers dig for lost hours.
I don't want any more nights of a black moon without you.
I don't want to have to include the hundred gallows
reflected in a crow's eye. In the Jewish cemetery
in Prague the crows scream from high trees
like no place else in the city. Below them,
the old synagogue is filled with pictures
by the fifteen thousand children of Terezin,
thousands of pictures of the lives
they tried to live beside the one in the camp,
the flowers, the ploughs and houses, the bright moons,
even the smiling Nazi guards, and the one picture,
drawn across an admission form, of a street sign
pointing to Prague in one direction, blank in the other.

Where did they think they were going? Maybe it is
no longer natural for the heart to take its usual place
in our breasts. Now it seems each flower is a lens
for seeing into a darker world. Maybe this is why
the moon seems to tumble around our planet
like a loaded die. Even the clock towers have begun
to remember a time when we talked freely with angels.
The new theory is that we carry a few Neanderthal
genes around in our biological pockets. Since then
we've tried to grow wings against each death.
This is the metaphor Plato used in his *Phaedrus*
for love. Another theory is that love and sex evolved
recently as a natural defense against parasites.

For me each leaf has a different dream.
When you dream whole armies fall asleep in your eyes.
I want to live again in the pine forests of your voice.
I don't want to stumble with someone else's moon
across the rooftops of some bombed town
dodging the crosshairs of despair.

I am watching two crows descend to a branch
like those eyelids you see in pictures from the camps.
I want, like Blake, to create a Heaven from Hell.
Haydn used to worry that the face in the moon was his.
The soldier with half a face fights the other half
everywhere. Here and there the night is
pulling up its collar and walking away.
I can almost make out the faint odor of stars.
I don't know whose shadow has taken the place of my own.
It is the bird with one wing that is singing my song.
It is my own face that is inscribed in the moon.

Terzanelle of Kosovo Fields

The soldier thinks he can beat the moon with a stick.
His is a country where roads do not meet, nor words touch.
The walls around him crumble: his heart is a pile of bricks.

We sit with the sky draped across our knees and trust
that the shadows of planes whisper like children in the fields,
follow roads that do not meet us, speak words we will not touch.

The soldier lights a fuse that makes a tragic story real:
our words scavenge the countryside like packs of dogs, derelict,
abandoned, hunted by the shadows of planes that cross the fields.

It's true that the blackbirds fill the air with their terrible music.
How could we think a soldier wouldn't turn our stars to sawdust?
Now our words scavenge the countryside, and our loves are derelict.

I wanted to love you beyond the soldier's aim, beyond the war's clutch.
Now bombs hatch in our hearts. Even the smoke abandons us for the sky.
How could we think a soldier wouldn't turn our stars to sawdust?

We live in a world where the earth refuses to meet the sky.
Our homes are on the march, their smoke abandons us for the sky.
Our soldiers thought they could beat the moon with their sticks.
Now every heart is crumbling, every love is a pile of bricks.

You Can't Get the Facts until You Get the Fiction

The fact is that the Death I put on in the morning is
the same Love I take off each night. The fact is
that my life slips out the back door just as I arrive.
Just now, just as I tell you this, while I am looking
for a little dignity under the open wound of the sky,
I am putting down the story of the two lovers killed
on a bridge outside Mostar. And the fact is love is
as extinct as those animals painted on cave walls
in Spain. The fact is, there is not a place on earth
that needs us. All our immortal themes are sitting
on the porch with woolen blankets over their knees.
But who wants to believe this? Instead, I am looking
for the right words as if they were hidden under
my doormat like keys. I would like to be able to report
that the nine year old Rwandan girl did not hide under
her dead mother for hours. There are so many things
too horrible to say. And I would like to tell you
the eyes of the soldiers are sad, that despite all
this madness I can still kiss your soul, and yes,
you might say I was angry if it were not for the plain fact,
the indisputable fact, that I am filled with so much love,
so much irrational, foolish love, that I will not take
the pills or step off the bridge because of the single
fact of what you are about to say, some small act
of kindness from our wars, some simple gesture that fools me
into thinking we can still fall, in times like this, in love.

II

                                        . . . don't scold
this art written by my other self, filled with confusion, not lies,
and forgive even this varied style I use now, that flies
darkly as the crow, that scans the secret life of the mole.
                          Petrarch

You need a style both grave and light.
                          Horace, Satire I.x
                          (trans. Matthews)

No Turn on Red

It's enough to make the moon turn its face
the way these poets take a kind of bubble bath
in other people's pain. I mean, sure, the dumpsters
of our lives are filling with more mistakes
than we could ever measure. Whenever we reach into
the pockets of hope we pull out the lint of despair.
I mean, all I have to do is lift the eyelids
of the stars to see how distant you could become.
But that doesn't mean my idea of form is a kind of
twelve-step approach to vision. I mean, I don't want
to contribute to the body count which, in our major journals,
averages 13.7 deaths per poem, counting major catastrophes and wars.
I'm not going to blame those bodies floating down some
river in Rwanda or Bosnia on Love's failures. But really,
it's not the deaths in those poems, it's the way Death arrives in a tux
and driving a Lamberghini, then says a few rhymed words
over his martini. It's a question of taste, really,
which means, a question for truth. I mean, if someone
says some beastly person enters her room the way Hitler
entered Paris I'd say she's shut her eyes like a Kurdish
tent collapsing under a gas attack, it makes about as
much sense. Truth is too often a last line of defense,
like the way every hospital in America keeps a bag
of maggots on ice to eat away infection when the usual
antibiotics fail. The maggots do a better job
but aren't as elegant. Truth is just bad taste, then?
Not really. Listen to this. "Legless Boy Somersaults
Two Miles To Save Dad," reads the headline from Italy
in *Weekly World News*, a story that includes pictures
of the heroic but bloody torso of the boy. "Twisted
like a pretzel," the story goes on. Bad taste or
world class gymnastics? Which reminds me. One afternoon
I was sitting in a bar watching the Olympics—the singles
of synchronized swimming—how can that be true?
If that's so, why not full contact javelin? Uneven
table tennis? The fifteen hundred–meter dive? Even the relay dive?
Someone's going to say I digress? Look, this is a satire
which means, if you look up the original Latin, "mixed dish,"—

you have to take a bite of everything. True, some would
argue it's the word we get *Satyr* from, but I don't like
to think of myself as some cloven-hoofed, horny little
creature sniffing around trees. Well, it's taste, remember.
Besides my satire is set while waiting at Love's traffic
light, which makes it unique. So, I was saying you have
to follow truth's little detours—no, no, it was taste,
the heroic kid twisted like a pretzel. Pretzels are
metaphysical. Did you know a medieval Italian monk
invented them in the year 610 in the shape of crossed,
praying arms to reward his parish children?
"I like children," said W.C. Fields—"if they're properly
cooked." Taste, and its fellow inmate, truth—how do we
measure anything anymore? Everyone wants me to stick
to a few simple points, or maybe no point at all,
like the tepid broth those new formalists ladle into their
demitasse. How can we write about anything—truth,
love, hope, taste, when someone says the moment, the basis
of all lyric poetry, of all measure and meter, is just
the equivalent of ten billion atomic vibrations of the cesium
atom when it's been excited by microwaves. Twilight chills
in the puddles left by evening's rain. The tiny spider
curled on the bulb begins to cast a huge shadow. No wonder
time is against us. In 1953, Dirty Harry, a "nuclear device,"
as the phrase goes, blossomed in Nevada's desert leaving
more than twice the fallout anyone predicted.
After thirty years no one admits the measurements.
Truth becomes a matter of "duck and cover." Even Love
refuses to come out of its shelter. In Sarajevo,
Dedran Smailovic plays Albinoni's *Adagio* outside
the bakery for 22 days where mortars killed 22,
and the papers are counting the days till the sniper
aims. You can already see the poets lined up on
poetry's drag strip revving up their 22-line elegies
in time for the *New Yorker's* deadline, so to speak.
Vision means, I guess, how far down the road of your
career you can see. And numbers not what Pope meant
by rhythm, but $5 per line. Pythagoras (b. 570 B.C.)
thought the world was made entirely of numbers. Truth,
he said, is the formula, and we are just the variables.
But this is from a guy who thought Homer's soul was

26

reborn in his. Later, that he had the soul of a peacock.
Who could trust him? How do we measure anything?
Each time they clean the standard kilogram bar in Sevres,
France, it loses a few atoms making everything else appear
a little heavier. That's why everything is suddenly
more somber. Love is sitting alone in a rented room
with its hangman's rope waiting for an answer
that's not going to come. All right, so I exaggerate, and
in bad taste. Let's say Love has put away its balance,
tape measure, and nails and is poking around in its tin
lunch pail. So how can I measure how much I love you?
Except the way the willow measures the universe.
Except the way your hair is tangled among the stars.
The way the turtle's shell reflects the night's sky.
I'm not counting on anything anymore. Even the foot—
originally defined as the shoe length of whatever king
held your life, which made the poets scramble around
to define their own poetic feet. And truth is all this?
That's why it's good to have all these details as
a kind of yardstick to rap across the fingers
of bad taste. "I always keep a supply of stimulants
handy," said Fields, "in case I see a snake;
which I also keep handy." In the end, you still need
something to measure, and maybe that's the problem
that makes living without love or truth so much pain.
I'd have to be crazy. Truth leaves its fingerprints
on everything we do. It's nearly 10 P.M. Crazy.
Here comes another poet embroidering his tragic
childhood with a few loosely lined mirrors.
I'm afraid for what comes next. The birds' warning
song runs up and down the spine of the storm. Who says
any love makes sense? The only thing left is
this little satire and its faceless clock for a soul.
You can't measure anything you want. The basis of all
cleverness is paranoia. 61 percent of readers never finish
the poem they start. 31 percent of Americans are afraid to speak
while making love. 57 percent of Americans have dreamt
of dying in a plane crash. One out of four
Americans is crazy. Look around at your three
best friends. If they're okay, you're in trouble.

Basic Algebra

What does it matter if six is not seven?
Morning takes off its blindfold and the night
breaks into tiny roaches that scamper into
the crevices behind my refrigerator.
I refuse to pay such high prices for vegetables.
I don't feel any need to apologize for the number
of breaths I will take today. I have no
excuses for my age which has approached
the starting point of Zeno's paradox. Whenever
I see three at the supermarket, reaching
for more than he can hold, the legs and arms
of his clothes too short, he is distraught,
terribly distraught, that he is not eight.
Every number pretends to account
for more than itself. Therefore
the truth of every figure is a paradox.
Eight is the most sensual of numbers
writes Joachim of Avalon, platonic pimp
for the great Petrarch. When he pulls the chord,
the corporal at the howitzer has already
double checked his figures for elevation
though in the end he resorts to trial and error.
It was a mistake to keep this single knife in my heart
so long, but it is my knife, and my heart, too,
with its four distinct chambers. The only thing
that saves me is the certain fact that one is
not a number. It leans against the subway wall
afraid to go on. It listens to no one
and no one listens to it. I am going to
build a new nest for each of the birds in my throat.
For every kind thing you say, my father would
always tell me, a hundred kind things are
visited upon you. This is despite the fact
that somewhere someone is keeping
a second set of books about our lives.
Despite the number of howitzer shells
stockpiled inside our dreams.

None of this should enter our equation.
Maybe we should think of another number
besides ten which we can base our math upon.
Lately, despite the fact that some branches
refuse to offer a flower, despite the sky's
eating away at the horizon, I have been
thinking of eleven, which is also a lovely number.

The Poem That Was Once Called "Desperate" But Is Now Striving to Become the Perfect Love Poem

So then the sunken heart was hauled up, nearly breaking
the nets, and just at that moment, back ashore,
while the scandalous flowers were opening to the sun,
while Agamemnon had finished sending his messages
of condolence to his wife, the somber moon
began to exert unusual control over this sentence,
and I thought, wait a minute, what if this poem worked
and she began to love me? What if I could invent
a new word the way Catullus invented a word
for kiss? And would I have time to change those stars
that have been embalmed in the eyes of Agamemnon
to something like—well,—but I know I *could*
think of something the way Clytemnestra's sentries
imagined every sunrise or glint of steel
to be the long-awaited signal fire.
Sentries, secret messages, royal scandals,
who am I kidding? When am I going
to stop living off the debris of lost loves?

But if it was to work, the poem, shouldn't I stop
wasting time and talk about something more
important in order to make her love me? There's
the Clytemnestra syndrome to think about here,
that is, the question of who lies best to whom.
And take Catullus,—in one of his poems to Lesbia,
he talks about Troy and Heracles just to let her know
how cultured he is—yes, the mind, despite what we think,
it's *that* important—and then he mentions his brother
who died in Turkey, and he really did mourn a lifetime
for him, but the point is, he lets Lesbia feel his remorse too,
then sympathy, then,—well, good sex, that was
Catullus's aim all along, wasn't it? And so with this
poem, surely there's time to add something about
my knowledge of the Trojan war, the complexities
concerning Agamemnon's murder of his daughter
and how I agree that, no matter how much the gods
commanded him, he should have turned around and
set sail for home and his anxious wife, all the while

emphasizing my essential sympathy with Clytemnestra's
plan to cut the bastard up like tonight's roast pork.

Maybe I should just go back to that little ship in the cove,
hauling up not a heart this time, but a statue, yes,
and an important find, good enough for a famous museum,—
but, well, maybe not, museums mean the past, death, lost
civilizations, lost love, so maybe a treasure,—okay, ancient
Greek coins because this poem is set off some Greek isle,—
Agamemnon, remember—but wait, the trouble with dragging
in Agamemnon is that Aeschylus who wrote the play died
on just such a shore when an eagle dropped a shell on his head—
so maybe it's Sappho's island—this sticks better to my subtext—
where the poetess mourned for her lost love, and where—

But Sappho, you ask? Okay, true enough, but remember
Catullus also filled his poems with confusions of gender
to suggest the largesse of his sensitive and empathetic
vision to even the most difficult of lovers. Me too.
And why should I keep my hormones padlocked
in a single shed? Look what happened to Clytemnestra
waiting a decade for the one thing that drove her mad.
And why does everyone have to keep frisking the heart
for secret weapons? Why should I have to live like
there's an asterisk next to my love? Maybe the desperate
past is ready to weigh anchor, maybe my ideas are so plentiful
they'll just spill from the holes in my pockets like ancient
coins, and there she'll be, on that shore as the boat sails off,
happy like me, dressed like a Greek goddess, and she's ready
to spend a little time in my story, this story, with you
and me, where love is smuggled on board in containers
marked history, responsibility, prophecy, all those things
Desire's watchman never sees, decorum, reason, reality,
and all the other contraptions we use to try to avoid them.

Liberation Theology

I feel suddenly liberated because Love has ripped
the maps from the walls of my brain and
because Despair no longer holds me like a rabbit
in its teeth. My thirteenth century manual describing
techniques for levitation says the earth is trying

to spin fast enough to cast us off anyway. Maybe I am
just in a state of pure and absolute grace.
I have learned to feel perfectly relaxed
when the stars no longer ask
for my help. In Torcello it wasn't the huge mosaic

of the last judgment that captured me but
the fact that I sat in Attila's stone chair
and watched the sun set like Western civilization
over the Venetian lagoon. I felt dizzy then with nothing
around me the way I felt when I climbed Vrsic,

seven thousand feet in the Slovene Alps, and the huge spaces
between the rock cliffs of the next mountains almost
sucked me into their secrets. I refused to be jealous of
Zeus on Olympus who could just yank a few clouds over
to lean upon. Maybe Love is just a disturbance

in the earth's magnetic field that throws us
off balance. Do we need to have needs? The stars
crave the darkness. The mockingbird never hears
its own song. Does the moon really require the earth
to tug at its sleeve? Zeus is the most oppressive figure

in Western civilization because he always points
the same way. Isn't there anyone who isn't so
tiresome? How about the great Italian
psychologist, Ficino, who wrote in his fifteenth century
Book of Life that we have to let the mind wander out

into dangerous spaces. And did you notice when
I said I was "captured" by the idea of Attila's
chair? What does that do to my feelings about liberation?
Maybe space is just a meaningless kiss. Maybe Jealousy
is just the workman climbing the telephone pole

to listen in on our intimate conversations. Can we still have
intimate conversations if we are even this liberated?
How distant must we be to call ourselves liberated
and independent? Pluto is so far out they are beginning
to think it is only one of the large asteroids that make

a sort of belt to keep us all tucked in here.
My own theory is that it has simply tired
of our neon hearts blinking on and off
throughout the night. Everyone who climbed up
with me has started down. Drinking beer

at this altitude is a lot less expensive. Why can't
the infinite explosions of stars be heard this high?
Is it really that hard to fly? Sometimes I think my heart
is full of the kind of graffiti that marks these cliffs.
Perhaps I am almost in my right mind.

It would be bad luck to say what is supposed to happen
when you sit in Attila's throne so I am not going to
resolve that part of this poem. In fact,
if I am so liberated I shouldn't have
to resolve anything, should I? Maybe I am on the next

mountain with the Zlatog, the name of a kind of
mountain goat with mythical powers to free you
from death and bring the kind of love that turns the seasons.
They skim the rock cliffs like water bugs.
It is also the name of the beer I am drinking

while waiting for Love to lean over the table and whisper
the one thing that will free me from being so liberated.
So what have I learned here? Petrarch climbed a mountain
and discovered that the meaning of Love is difficulty.
Maybe I should have chosen Epicurus, not the obscure Ficino

or the reckless Attila, or the thoroughly whipped Petrarch.
Epicurus held his philosophy classes in a garden
to foster feelings about the infinite lushness of the world.
The waiter brings more beer. Everything looms larger.
My Love will be back any moment. Potato soup, with onions and paprika.

Benediction

Briefly, that my petition for sainthood has been denied is
an outrage. What should it matter that my life has been
hidden like those wall paintings in undersea caves that were once
hillside sentries far from any shore? I remember the hunters
returning to trace their hands over a stag or boar to claim
its soul. Each cave was a shrine, each death a sacrament.
Whenever they prayed, the green stars fell like leaves.
When we peel away the night from the sky it leaves only
another night.

                  But I digress. Nor do I see any need to defend
the absence of relics or miracles "of a certain kind." They are
like the old movie tickets you find in a pocket, or the cosmologies
of Pliny who died trying to investigate the eruptions of Vesuvius.
Better science could have told you that your arcane theories
cannot be verified. I have argued that Love is the only prayer,
the only science. I could argue the obvious—that there is no
objectivity or balance in this world. Even the North Pole has shifted
two feet to the West because of the weight of new reservoirs
which are concentrated in the northern hemisphere, thus
tilting the planet. It's like we're on this giant pinball machine
that says *Game Over*. We're already spinning two hundred–millionths
of a second slower per year because of the moon's pull. Before long
we will never be able to spin back to where we began, and,
according to recent calculations, all time will stop.

                                         Which is why
even now we have too much leisure time, hence the recent breakdown
in our moral fiber. That too is an outrage. Why couldn't you accept me
as your saint? Even eternity starts checking its wristwatch at the local
cab stand. How little time we have had. Tomaz says that too many
blessings break a man apart. He and Maggie showed me Cranach's
painting of deer herded like lovers, like hearts, into the walled garden
to be slaughtered. In the hills of Kosovo the snipers are reloading.

How little time. Whenever we refused each other we peeled
a little skin from the soul. Listen, everyone is a saint, but buzzards

circle their words. Do you hear what I am saying? It is raining
inside my dream of you. The only true saints won't let the heart
raffle off their desires. Once we could trust the simple spinning
of the planet to bring us back. But to where? The bees follow
a pathway in the air. The bear follows its own scent back to the cave.
Even the martyrs learn how to avoid Despair's henchmen.

And if we do return we find our towns abandoned, our best
memories forced to the road by the tanks of some jealousy
that point like compass needles. Why should we be a part
of any argument the stars have with infinity? Is there any end
to your theories, your histories of the heart? Is there
any way we can purely touch the world again, the way
a salamander does, breathing through its skin? Can we
become the strands of this shrine we weave ourselves into
hoping to emerge into a world where—where what?
There is no end to desire, which means no end to regret,
no end to our need for an ending, so that even the sky refuses
our touch, that sky which, at is bluest, is the most empty.

No Fault Love

No one seeing the suspect, Richard Jackson, should ever
try to approach him. His description contains as many
contradictions as Proteus. The heart's cabdriver
reports that he has fled into tomorrow because he is so
tired of speaking about yesterday. If you do not
recognize his crime you are already an accomplice.
The remarkable thing about tomorrow is that everything is
the opposite of today. The shadow that now stalks you
becomes your confessor. And it is true, Desire never
loses its grip on tomorrow. But just because tomorrow
follows today does not necessarily mean that one thing
always follows another. The bullet that is heading
for your heart may never arrive, the plane floundering
toward earth may even pull up at the last minute,
given the ambiguities and uncertainties of tomorrow.
None of tomorrow's verbs can ever finish what they're doing.
Trees stand for anything. Stars, too, stand for anything.
The whole galaxy screams something that is soon forgotten.
So you can forget about the Bosnian bells with their
human tongues. The business of tomorrow is pulling up
the roots of sadness so that the three children
blown up in the speed factory in San Diego—
what am I saying? We want to live as if our own bodies
were nests. But possibility opens like the palm of
a waving dictator. You can scale the ruins of heaven
in search of love and never find it. But if you find
Richard Jackson tomorrow, or even the day after,
approach with caution—his words are snares.
The horrible thing about tomorrow is that today is already
history. We don't even exist the way we exist.
Truth becomes a fixture. Love wakes in the keyholes.
I don't know what other clues to give you.
All the good souls have fallen from their nests.
By tomorrow, the scene of the crime will be forgotten.
But the heart, the heart's fingerprints are everywhere.

My Black Madonna

Don't worry, on this night of decapitated stars,
on this night when someone has already broken
into the cash box of desire, when time has dealt
its cards out face down, I'm not going to
beg you for prayer pledges for whatever you can
afford, I'm not going to reach my hand
toward the camera and ask you to touch the TV
for salvation or some miracle that will call back all
your wayward cells. I know you, too, have
some place to be in a few minutes. There are thousands
of miracles squatting around the dull fires
of one promise or another, some votive
candle in a dark chapel, just waiting
for someone to bring more kindling, a dumb war
or natural catastrophe that brightens everyone's faces.

The past sticks to their fingers like money.
Sometimes they sit around the Loretto chapel
which lights up in Prague like a Chinese lantern.
Inside, you can see the *Santa Casa*, modeled
on Mary's house which several industrious angels
flew from Nazareth to Yugoslavia to Italy
and a few other stopovers a few centuries back.
They must have filled the night sky like Dali's
flaming giraffes. Inside the shrine is a Black Madonna,
but not the one I found in Prague above a corner
just outside the old square where the monument
to Jan Hus shows the hero rising
from a mass of bodies and pointing to the horizon
he called freedom. We had just finished
a few cinnamon crepes. The future was hanging

some political banners and making last minute
adjustments to the stage. My Black Madonna
watches over everything from a gold cage
just as she has since the early seventeenth century.
She does not sit on anyone's dashboard.
I confess I cursed her coyness when I couldn't
find her at first. That was when my soul was

at the other end of the square bargaining
with some local merchants. Brad, Karri,
and Danielle were trying to find some doorway
to hide under. Jenn said our souls would never even
sneak across the border into the promised land.
We could all see another revolution leaning
seductively against a billboard, its bags
at its feet, checking its tickets, fingering a few coins.

My Black Madonna knows all about history's
leaky faucet. She knows all about those stars
whose hymns everyone claims at funeral time.
So don't worry, there aren't going to be any requiems
for lost comrades in the manner of our more
sensitive poets who sit around in the vestibules
of the heart like those shipwrecked sailors
Persius says begged the streets of Rome
with enough emotion to break your heart
and purse. When he died at twenty-eight, Persius left
a few unfinished poems, unlike, say,
Catherine of Siena who left her own
perfectly preserved head. I saw it once in her
not so modest house, but that's really another story
in another poem of mine you might read, if you care,—

fine print, good papers, not too expensive. But
I was starting to talk about my Black Madonna
and I don't want to hold you up too long
like Coleridge's guilt ridden wedding guest.
Today you can see a lot of sincere Religious Truths
cleaning their weapons under the shade of a fig tree,
the sweat just beginning to show under their arms,
or maybe hammering down some Indian or Pakistani
mosque or temple, or flying their jets, which after all,
nearly take the shape of some of our fancier crosses.
My Black Madonna's been trying to say something
about the tortures and camps in Bosnia, and it is
true—some victims are shipped to meat plants,
or burnt like fourth of July bonfires.
She is not going to leave a saucer of pity

for you to lap up. She does not ask the breath
to be soul, nor ask the numbers to fall
from their clocks. She does not demand
some crystal cathedral. Yet, if it were not for her
touch the moon would not cover herself each month.
The triple heartbeat of the octopus is nothing
compared to hers. My Black Madonna has not
forgotten Jan Hus for his religious vision,
though now the Czechs see him
only as some patriotic symbol.
From one side it looks like he's hailing a cab.
Our own ride should be along any minute.
Should I put on a new herringbone jacket for dinner?
When I met my Black Madonna the famous
astronomical clock on the town hall

had just failed to perform for the first time
so I never got to see Death, Greed, and Vanity
prepare for the same cock that crowed for Saint Peter,
never saw it flap its wooden wings and send me
home like a street vendor whose dreams
dangle from the torn lining of his coat.
It was from Jan Hus that we get the word
anarchy. I no longer believe in the fruitless
quest of clocks to capture tomorrow.
In fact, we already live in a past some
sincere fanatic's bomb will make of us.
Across the square chimney smoke is
following the paths of several previous saints.
So it's true, the future is the last refuge of the sincere.
A little south, where the moon is only

the broken shell of a beetle, where my Black Madonna
first entered Europe a few centuries ago,
my friend Tanya must be watching her Sarajevo
take the same path. Maybe she is still
wearing her long leather coat, trying
the doors of illegal bars after hours. Poems there
no longer fit any locks and dangle
at the poets' sides like custodians' unused keys.
They are hiding out in dark cellars from snipers.

All the guns of that town are pushing back their chairs
and rising once again from the table, patting
their stomachs. Each of them has their own
religion that comes rubbing up against them
like a cat looking for leftovers. Their fugitive
angels are waiting for boxcars in the railroad yards,

waiting in bus stations, trying as always to make do
with our hand-me-down clothes and histories.
Back here in Prague, the late hour straightens
its necktie ready to keep the usual appointments.
I wish my Black Madonna would do something
about all this. But this is the way it always is.
Even Hus was burned at the stake in 1415.
We're supposed to be at dinner in thirty minutes.
Most of Persius's friends were killed or exiled.
I hope the chardonnay is chilled correctly.
In the end the heart is just a night watchman
punching a time clock in an empty warehouse.
Even Forgiveness has his own collection plate.
The wind begins to feel like an orphan.
Someone else steps into the cab Destiny had hailed.

Decaf Zombies of the Heart

For several hours now, for several days and maybe
even weeks, while Regret kept licking
the stamps, while Despair lost the letters,
while I forgot to feel the door
of this burning satire before opening it,
for several hours, I mean tonight, this very night, I watch
in horror as these decaf zombies stumble
through the heart's heavy traffic, how their touch
drifts off like the smoke from our cigarettes,
how each word they speak loses
its place in the unread narratives of each wart
and cut, each lost love or mystic vision
of their lives. Tonight, of all nights,
when the stars are louder
than I have ever remembered, when the grass listens
so attentively, I have this desperate
desire to kiss the dark side of the moon,
to play only the broken string
of your violin, to kiss your anger on its forehead, your pain
on its lips, and I have this desperate desire
to jimmy open your heart like an amateur thief, and maybe
it is my own manic soul chasing you
down the corridors of the past that makes me
so impatient with a poet who can imagine the end of beauty,
or whose Love dozes off in an empty bus station waiting
for a ride anywhere, or whose poems
dance through magazines like electric ballerinas
but whose heavy words clog the arteries of each last line.
Tonight I have the greatest impatience for those love poets
whose words moan from bar stools like dull
politicians nodding the world into another war.
How their stars blink like the muzzles of guns!
How they doze to the sounds of a screaming bomb!
Tonight, I'm going to find a poem that somersaults
through your soul like a desperate circus performer.
Tonight I feel sorry for those decaf zombies
who only turn over in sleep when a siren or dog
announces its own risky self, whose tired arms
fall across the breasts of their lovers like ice-bound trees.

Tonight, I'm going to rev up the jukebox of desire.
I'm going to take a pickax to the grave of every abandoned feeling.
Tonight I want to drive the back roads of your dreams
looking for a house to break into, forgetting the heart's
land mines, and I want to step carelessly everywhere
tonight of all nights, still awake, and after
so many days, and even weeks after
the clocks have walked off like innocent bystanders,
because maybe there is only the shell casing of
this moment about to shatter, or maybe it is
just morning rounding the corner like a door-to-door salesman—
whatever he's selling I'm buying. I tell you,
the way I feel the sky better put on its armor. In my dreams
the phone is ringing or someone knocks
at the door. There is an open window at the end
of each sentence for you. Maybe I am
only that quarter moon pinching a star awake
over your shoulder—*do you hear me?*—
taking my words from libraries
of the wind, my dreams from the heart's barracks,
but sensing, too, the sound of your soul
arriving before you do, the way, as a boy, I'd lay my head
down on the track not to sleep, but to listen for approaching trains.

Having a Drink with the Gods

This, finally, is the poem with the important message.
Not the meteors dissolving like mothballs. Not the cold
that is so clumsy it is breaking flowers and galaxies.
Not even Circe who you find on any corner with an armful
of wristwatches, nor Persephone's mother selling pretzels
across the street. These old gods, you know them, they want
to be like the chickadees that grow new brain cells
each October to remember where they planted their seeds.

And us? We live in a world that's trying to harvest
the lost sperm of Woolly Mammoths and dinosaurs.
The place we are is never the place we are. I looked
for you under a sky whose arteries had hardened.
Like the early philosophers, I wanted our sight to originate
in our eyes. I wanted to believe Aphrodite could fashion
a whole world out of love's fires. I wanted to forget those
quantum theories about sub-atomic deaths that haunt

our lives. Maybe this is why I am so worried about microbes.
Last night in our seedy restaurant, I kept thinking
how five million bacteria per gram is considered safe,
that if all the microbes of the world were dried and stacked
they would cover France three feet thick. Oh,—that important
message? How else do you think I could have gotten you
to listen to me? At one time the secret of this poem was
that it reproduced, in every detail, our first moments together.

In my recurring dream someone knocks at the door
and wakes me up. Sometimes I spend half the night
answering the emptiness, hoping it is you. Memory is just
another form of imagination. Now the glasses are empty.
A future flies into the rafters. Daylight leaks into my dream.
Eventually I may have to write a love poem to myself
like the great Hungarian poet, Atilla Jozsef (1905–1937),
counting shooting stars over the Danube for over sixty years now.

The Sentimental Poem I Almost Didn't Write

I fell out of my dream at 3:00 A.M. like that medieval monk
who would land in trees and have
to be rescued with ladders. That's why I found myself
talking to the birds that have made a nest behind
the broken screen of my bathroom window. Yesterday I watched
the mother feed a cricket to one of the fledglings
and I thought for a moment that we could both fly out
among the restless stars over the enormous gully of 3:01 A.M.
When you left, two hawks crossed the road in front of me
as if they were making love in mid-air
and then melted into the Slovene woods. Sometimes I think
birds fly from your fingers when you touch me
and make their way toward places I can't see.

Now the wind is lifting the eyelid of the lake.
I remember my soul breaks open like a seed beneath
the ground just to think of you. Now it is 3:02 A.M.,
a time when my dreams often migrate to the desert where
they pitch their tents like Bedouins and the desert blooms.
I remember how carefully you point the camera toward
the least flower as if somehow you held the universe in its lens.

I am sorry my words sometimes frighten
the fireflies from your dreams. I am sorry that battalions of doubt
have pitched camp in your heart. It would be crazy to love you
as much as I do. It is 3:03 and by now the whole universe is
attracted to you so that I feel gobbled up like the ice in a comet.

I am sorry the time is passing so slowly.
I am sorry, birds, for not mentioning you again until the end.
My fifth grade teacher said comets are angels.
You can determine the exact makeup of a comet
by spectrographic analysis. An X ray of this poem would reveal
dark spots on its heart. It would reveal the smallest memories—
my hand resting so gently on your hip that it requires
great effort just to stay on this earth,
how your legs seem to become
part of your bicycle and you seem to fly into a world
that lies beside this one. I am sorry that now, at 3:04 A.M.,

I have already become too sentimental. I am sorry I lost a draft
of this poem in the Campo Dei Fiori where we had supper
last week in the shadow of the statue of Giordano Bruno.
He was burned there a few hundred years ago for writing
that there might be life on other worlds.

There is no end to what we humans can do to each other.
In Vienna, someone has finally decided to bury
the brains of the four hundred children the Nazi doctors killed
in some experiment to find their young dreams.
When Berkevic gave me the copies of poems from Bosnian
orphans he was working with, I completely broke.
That was just a few hours ago before the storm rolled down
out of the mountains. Even the stars were confused.
It is 3:06, but I am six hours ahead of your time.
In a storm the birds will fly backwards and suddenly
it is ten minutes ago, and I am still dreaming of you.
Sometimes it is fifty years and we think we can change history.
Each breath we take is a magnet, each word a point on the compass.
Sometimes we are five minutes too late.

I am starting to wake again. Don't give up on me. I realize
if I were any kind of saint I would not be the kind that lands in trees,—
and I wouldn't be Saint Francis of Assisi
with his sackcloth tunic and stigmata the way I was
in the fifth grade pageant, nor one of the birds he talked to,
resting at your window, not meaning a thing, crazy for love,
for this night, even when I didn't know you, only the possibility of you.

III

They flee from me, that sometime did me seek,
With naked foot, stalking in my chamber:
I have seen them gentle tame and meek,
That now are wild, and do not remember
That sometime they put themselves in danger
To take bread at my hand; and now they range,
Busily seeking with continual change.

                  . . . but once in special,
In thin array, after a pleasant guise,
When her loose gown from her shoulders did fall,
And she me caught in her arms long and small,
Therewithal sweetly did me kiss,
And softly said, "dear heart, how like you this?"

                        Sir Thomas Wyatt

Heartless Poem

It is true that my heart does not exist.
It is absolutely true that the birds are not mine,
the river will not stop for me, the leaves will not
stop aiming for the very ground where I stand,
that I cannot hold the smallest amount of air
in my hands. The closed fist of the moon
punches its way through the lake.
Someone else might talk about the moon as a heart,
but that's all I'm going to say about it.
On this night when the stars begin their lies
about the light beyond them, when the young men
from Tuzla are hanging from lamp posts
instead of lights, I am here to tell you
my heart has never existed.
The only feelings I have ever heard of
take to the highway with the carts
and trucks of the other refugees.
Why do you think you need to join them?
If it were a violin my heart would not rest
between anyone's chin and shoulder. It would
sit in a pawnshop window for someone's supper.
On this night when my heart does not exist,
I eat out of the hands of yesterday.
If it did exist, the fist of my heart would
grab the hanged man by the collar of his soul
and turn him away from his own death.
But who can say anything about the soul?
The soul, too, is just another migrant.
I have heard that the soul and the heart are
the two best scavengers of whatever past
you have discarded by the side of the road.
You can find them sneaking around in some orchard
behind the smoke a farmer uses against the frost
or plucking the hanged man's weight like a pear.
See, it is not so hard to say something about nothing.
The stars are already leaking their light into dawn.
But I can tell you that my own heart has never existed.
That's all I'm going to say about it.

Grammar Rules

How absolutely confusing and yet how wonderful
to live this posthumous life, I mean
this absolutely preposterous love,
this fragrant life trying to be the verb in which we bloom,
this defoliated life that is the adjective by which we die,
this feathered life which means our participles gliding
over the fringes of passion, this vanished life
which means the perfectly imperative sentences
of the tank commander targeting two boys
who are perhaps kicking a soccer ball in a Sarajevo street,
these lives which are the ant trails of someone's narrative,
this language bursting at the seams of conscience
which is to say, of love, of hate, of clauses
revving up in the pit, phrases tumbling over the guardrail,
and how easily these lives avoid each other like crates
of history loaded and unloaded on the docks,
and how odd, how terribly odd that the doors
to my old words have been nailed tight, and yet
how wonderful that those same words recall the mindless
repetitions of the owl, the same owl you heard
outside my bedroom window with its unmade bed,
which means that maybe instead of talking
the way I am talking, which is the way I am thinking
in only a few scattered parts of speech
like a nervous schoolboy, maybe instead
I should be holding your smiling hands,
the very hands that once gripped the bottoms
of my lungs, those hands and their budding souls,
their nail polish, their outposts in my heart,
their choir of senses, their frying pans,
their fire, their mortar shells landing in the suburbs
of memory, their cats, their pills, their archangels,
their prison camps, their chocolate,
their discontent, their forests,
so maybe I am lucky that I do not live
my life as Richard Jackson but as this noun
that has to constantly be modified, which is to say
immortal, pungent, shuddering, theoretical,

this noun that beside you turns
resonant, clumsy, presumptuous, forged,
this life that is hovering or falling,
singing or weeping, but also breathing, yes breathing,
so in some ways alive, still waiting for you,
still taking cover in your invisible closets,
still thinking how impossibly sooner, how in between,
how never, because, too much, closer, inside you,
before, after, however, when, always, in spite of
this terrible love, these speechless shores,
only, every, beneath, meanwhile, now and forever.

Job's Epilogue

The stars prowled my skin but all I wanted
in the end was to see his face. I never doubted
when the rivers that I knew as him dried up.
Why did he want to stay so hidden? Blake says
you can see him in every grain of sand. There is
a million mile high tornado wandering through
the Lagoon galaxy that might be him. There are
these icicles reaching desperately for the earth
that may also be him. Now all I see is an old man
called Death standing under the storefront light
across the street clipping his nails. Does it matter?
All love turns into a beetle in the end. You have
to crush the shell with your heel to survive.
My own friends were a broom to any hope.
They watched me pass through time like a body
caught under the thickening ice until spring.
They tossed their words like salt on my garden.
They called themselves allies but they were planting
the explosives of revenge like terrorists.
They wanted to grab my soul by its throat.
Now they are rolling up your field maps,
looking for a destiny shaped like a conquerable
country, shaped even like the Afghan boy
whose hands have been cut off for stealing
food, like the girl nailed to the door in Bosnia.
Their words siphoned the air around me until
there was only stone. I could see the moon
turn its back to me. I could see the empty trains
leaving the camps. They wanted to leave me
lying dead on my own body. My soul was
playing tug-of-war with the wind. There was never
any meaning to any of it was what the beetles knew.
I'm not saying you don't have any choice, but
we get poured out like milk, then thicken like curds.
In the end, all we can drink are our own regrets.
If we were pieces of straw we'd be hunted down.
Their armies are toppling minarets and burning churches.
What good is it to let our thoughts burn like a naked

bulb in the prisoner's room? Eternity has a few more
words to say. I have more than I ever had, but less.
I could see the birds falling from my trees like leaves.
I could see my cup filling with shadows. I could see
the sun was only another kind of cage. What did
he think I would do with all I saw? Hope put away
its watch. Whenever I asked, his ears were full
of darkness. He thought I wanted to harness the stars.
He thought I wanted to teach the grasshopper to leap.
All I wanted in the end was to see his face. You can
hear each new idea rumbling over the horizon. It is written
somewhere that I am each one of you, that the moths
of despair have eaten away our desires, that our hopes
have turned to scar tissue and harden, but it isn't true.
We have to understand the sunlight as a way to cast shadows.
We have to touch each others' shadows like our own.
We have to understand each heart is a kind of cave.
We have to let the bats of hatred fly out of those caves.

Villanelle of the Crows

Your shadow whispered into mine as into the inner ear of snow,
though this morning I could dream we were never really there:
the Heart sometimes panics, stumbling to fly off with the crows.

Clouds breaking into crumbs, words blown away with the snow,
and the moon, your shadow's moon, a clove of garlic against despair—
and your shadow, too, losing its balance in the inner ear of snow.

Why does everything pretend only what the moon chooses to show?
Moonlight with its arm around your waist, moonlight of your hair—
but my dull Heart would tear Love's carrion, dive in with the crows.

Why is it that the snow never covers what we finally owe?
Why is the Heart always stumbling around in the soul's cold cellars?
Why was I waiting, angry—or suddenly filled with the fear of snow?

I was wrong. Everything we do only hides another guilt, or sows
a guilt that blooms white like a knife whose glint blares
across the fields, or startles a smile that turns the color of crows.

I have been watching the few stars spin cobwebs of cloud that glow.
I should have stayed. Maybe Love is just the shotgun blast in the air.
Tonight the empty air whispers. I myself am the inner ear of snow.
The Heart freezes. Words crack. Your Love flies off with the crows.

New and Selected Posthumous Poems

It's sad to think of Schopenhauer sleeping with a gun.
The shadows in his room are penitent. He's grieving
because he walked down one Berlin avenue searching
for another woman who'll reject him, and so missed an entire
set of possibilities on the next street. Choices. Choices.

He's afraid an enemy is going to emerge from a world
he forgot to look at. If only he knew that because
the photons of light that reflect us split into infinite worlds,
because the electron, say, falling from your scarf, the one
you left as a farewell gift, its red wool, leads everywhere
at once, the only question is which world we die in. The heart
sells its pencils on the corner of one. The owl comforts
the weeping trees in another. I never know why they are
weeping.

               Maybe for the boy who is tossing the frisbee
that is also the moon looking in on the sleeping Schopenhauer.
I am happy with my metaphysical relationship to the moon.
The boy has no idea that he is the man in Decani, Kosovo,
who stuffs the bodies he has shot into village wells
repeating the earliest form of germ warfare. They no
longer have to retrieve the bodies in the parallel world
of moonlight. The far edge of the field rises into a flock
of birds. Their song wants to be the sky. The sky wants
to be the earth. I think that is why the man from Bela Crkva
wants his picture taken with the father he just unearthed,
thinking he is still alive in his separate life.

                              Schopenhauer
watches as the moon skids off the road. The boy picks it up
because he sees it is an arrowhead or a piece of pottery.
The huge orb weaver wrapping his web between the bush
and the light pole like a thin scarf collects the light that seeps
from one world to another.

               Every loss begins another fiction.
In your world I have put down this poem, closed Schopenhauer,

and talked to Iztok about the war. In another I am dreaming
of the lover who really does appear at my door just now.
She must be you. And you, my love, through all these lives,
how long may I live in the obscure meanings of the words
you use to hold me, those words that can read the palms of
our souls, that let no night censor their wishes, this love
against which no war, no weeds of the heart, no galaxy
spiraling toward oblivion, no suspicions, no despair,
no sniper scope of fear, no parallel history, no photons
of memory, no accidental life smeared across our faces,
no death, no kiss could ever abandon or betray.

Cassandra's Litany

To see a solitary owl unlock the sky
and picture a whole army of regrets about
to emerge from the woods. To see Truth rise
in the face of your lover like the late winter sap.
To see everything from the carriage—the dagger,
the cloak that caught my Agamemnon like a fishnet
as if he were one of your common dictators.
To see your own heart split
open like a melon beside him. Also: to hate him
with the ferocity of love. To know we sometimes have to
invent a pain to love. To fear that love.
To spread love's deadly nets. To set its traps.
To open history's toolbox, to be there with the bomber
leaving his own future on a street in Mostar.
To have every word you toss into the darkness be sniped at
by bats. To cut yourself on the knife tips of stars
like the heart's assassin. To wait with the sniper
above Sarajevo, the way I saw Orestes crouching
like a lion behind a future he never understood.
To see his own regret straining like a bowstring.
To see the soldiers bayoneting the morning
to a chorus of history that never stops singing.
To see these victorious soldiers feasting
on the roasted flesh of tomorrow's children.
To know all these characters called Ajax
raping what they don't understand from Troy
to the second page of tomorrow's newspaper.
To know which asteroid, which microbe
will cross your path tomorrow. To look for hope
in this petri dish of a heart. Oh, to wash the bloody
walls of executions with a simple sponge!
To place your life in a tree top like one of your
Cherokee warriors so that it won't be stolen in battle.
To have your desires tattooed on a butterfly's wing.
To be believed. To be heard.
To know today's approaching gods for the butchers they are.
To leave this poem. To walk out among the meteors.
To lie down with anyone out of pure love.
To hear the nightingale and only hear a bird.
To understand, oh, to understand how in this world
a falling star could be a sign for joy.

No Man's Land

Where your heart opens like the pocket
watch of the artillery commander.
Where the road hoards its destination.
Where the weather vane of your heart turns away.
The extinct hearts of the animals we evolved from.
Where your doubts roam the streets, stalked
by impossible reasons. The heart does not break,
but shrivels like an orange on the table of the executioner.
Where the stars are set out against the sky like a string of mines.
Where everything is miles from itself.
Where each breath, without you, rusts like buckshot
in the lungs of the doe. Where even your best intentions
drag the lake of the past for what is left of my love.
Where my hopes cling like bats to your chimney walls.
Even a heart the size of a peach pit knows the pain it inflicts.
Each rose a heart, each heart a lifetime of sorrow.
It is February, but the heart says no, the month
that has been lost from ancient Babylonian calendars.
Where the stars of tiny suicides still try to flicker out.
Where the heart pinches them between its index finger and thumb.
Jude Thaddeus, patron of hopeless cases,
who disappeared on a mission into Syria
after writing his brief epistle—*clouds without rain*,
he wrote, while the wavering heart shriveled on the desert floor.
Where was it where the stars first melted in my hand
like the pills of the suicide no one could stop?
Where despair plays hopscotch up and down the discs of my spine.
The words zeroing in, the pattern of shell holes.
Is it so hard to believe we have been looking at the same moon?
In Zepa, Bosnia, the moon itself thins with hunger before
its belly bloats like a starving child.
As if the heart whispered a word it was ashamed of.
Why is the heart never as old as we are?
Except those hearts, remember, of tiny animals
preserved for millions of years in amber.
Where love hides in the attic, the closet,
the old trunks of my dreams.
Where the heart weighs anchor, where the soul rots
in the forgotten holds, in the leaking cargo bays,

where this death of mine lingers like a stowaway.
The heart's nightmare: dying in the arms of a stranger,
or dying on the tongue of consolations.
In the court of love Justice is ready with its leg irons.
Where Jude argues the losing case for hope.
Where reason ladles out its usual platitudes to the heart.
Where love knocks on the door with his blind man's cane
no one will hear but the two cats of conscience
who look up for a moment from playing with my bootstraps.
Where there are raindrops no one will listen to.
What it has come down to: the heart
of the Aztec warrior held above his empty chest,
still beating in the hands of the priest.
Where Death juggles our hearts like a bad circus performer.
Where the shadow of the suicide wanders the empty house.
Where the heart's map lies crumpled on your empty seat.
Scouring the want ads for the hearts no one wants.
The heart's park bench, love sleeping under the old papers,
Jude, too, there among the homeless, heart of bone, heart
of feathers, the compass heart spinning wildly,
the bridges of the heart collapsing, so that the stranded heart
checks into a cheap motel with its neon *vacancy*
keeping time to the pulse, hoping to decide between the pills
and the razor, but all the time praying, dear Jude, dear Jude,
print this place on all her signposts, let the clock resist the hour,
only to hold like falling snow her love in his arms.

Sonata of Love's History

Before I could arrive at this moment when the earth
wakes inside you, when the night is still tangled in your hair,
before I could see how the moonlight melts
on your breasts as you lay beside me,
before you opened the hands of your soul,
at this moment that is so sudden, so unexpected,
I can only imagine how the softness of your voice must be
enough to stop the insects for miles, and I begin
to understand how the way you open your eyes
to the morning must be enough to change orbits of planets,
so it must have been necessary for me, if I've really arrived
at this moment alive, to have lived
a life where only my shadow planted the garden,
only my shadow walked through the market,
fingered the keys nervously, drove the car too fast,
and it must be the same shadow that curls up
in the corner of the room or is hung in the closet
collecting moths, and it must have taken centuries
of bones turning to light, of rivers changing course,
of battles won or lost, of a farmer planting one crop
or another that failed or not, one atom hitting
another atom by chance, and through all this a single
string of time survived volcanoes, lightning strikes,
car wrecks, floods, invasions, to lead to this moment
abandoned randomly to us, this singular moment that is
part of time's litter or maybe its architecture, because now
in this moment which is so wondrous the way
it lies beside you, I either do not exist or the past
has never existed, either my breath is
the breath of stars or I do not breathe as I turn to you,
as you breathe my name, my heart,
as the net of stars dissolves above us, as you wrap
yourself around me like honeysuckle, the moon
turning pale because it is so drained by our love,
so that before this moment, before you lay beneath me,
you must have disguised yourself the way the killdeer
you pointed out diverts intruders to save what it loves,
pretending a broken wing, giving itself over finally
to whatever forces, whatever love, whatever touch,
whatever suffering it needs just to say I am here,
I am always here, stroking the wings of your soul.

Jeremiah's Lament

They said my voice was the storm that gathers in the flower.
They said my words covered the fields like locusts.
Whatever they said, I never wanted to stand apart, even
when they buried me under stones shaped from their hearts.
Yes, midnight clung to my lips, yes inside my mouth the stars
trembled, but who really listened? All they heard was
their own guilt crying inside them like caged birds.
Did what I say come true? Evil lurked in their wells.
God picked them clean the way a shepherd picks his cloak
clean of vermin. In the end, they gasped for air like jackals.
And truth in all this? You yourself have your physics
for the world,—quarks, for example, a matter of
mere logic to some, a real image to others. It only matters
that you believe. You have your own histories
strangling you like vines. For instance, 1597: the year
of the first military field hospitals, the year Spain
and France began peace talks, or the year Samurai warriors
brought back barrels filled with a hundred thousand noses and ears
from Korea to Kyoto. In Mostar they are still digging under
the rubble of someone's false prophecy. They are looking
for the truth that bursts from a hand grenade. We listen
only to history's megaphone, not the words that splinter
on whispers. We are all turning on a potter's wheel.
I wanted words that would laugh and weep at once,—
the fig trees that ripen as the mountains tremble,
the wolves of our desire whose voice flowers in the forest.
But these are the words that put me in jail, words
that lashed my own back, that seared my eyes, words that
still nest in the desert cactus. You call it beautiful, but
the song of the nightingale is only the pain
of never finding its own voice. Still,
everything speaks if you listen closely enough:
the desert dunes sing and moan, shout and stammer
under the weight of their own shifting sands, bees
make a map of air currents by beating their wings.
And my dreams? I dreamt God's judgment
in an almond rod, the city as a boiling pot, and I am
still waiting to see what they mean. I was
promised a bronze-walled city to protect me.

I was promised that the doors of Love would fly open.
Foggy with desire, we have to make our own truths.
All I can tell you is how it is your most precious Hope
that catches on the brambles, that blooms with each rain.
Imagine the stars filling the bottom of your glass.
I swear to you, the sun surrendering itself to darkness
beyond the tree line is the most poignant of moments.

Not Surprised

On your last day the aspen don't do anything
special, the hawks continue down the flyway,
a serviceman comes around to read the meter,
the garbage is picked up, the blinds, as usual,
need adjusting, the squirrels go on anyway
with their nests in the attic, the girl from across
the street rides her bike in the driveway, and the stars
that are hidden by daylight stay hidden by daylight.

Of the four men who stood one early evening
while the November stars gathered like frost
on the windows of the bar, while the crows argued
out back twenty years ago for kitchen scraps,
I'm the only one alive. I learned each death
years later,—by sniper, by land mine, by friendly
fire. It is with disbelief that I can touch
my own hand, my own face, or turn to touch you.

Anyone who expects archangels or lightning is fooled.
As long as the hawks soar, as long as the girl
will ride, as long as someone adjusts the blinds,
as long as the stars alone seem to fill the night,
no one believes you. But there you are, alive,
like me, and maybe that's enough. I could tell you.
Four men. Better to leave it like this, letting
Squirrels nest, the meter continue to count. Three.

Buy One, Get One Free

Federal regulations require that all passengers be
seated before we push away from the gate. You are
allowed two pieces of carry-on luggage, which must fit
in the overhead bin or beneath the seat in front of you.
According to the award level of your Frequent Flyer
membership when you buy this ticket, you get the second
one free. That's why I have taken you along so readily.
The question in packing is what to leave out.
The word *metaphor* comes from a Greek word having
to do with transportation. Even this poem is a sort of
journey. If you only knew what I left out. How long
I watched you the way the moon watches the earth.
The way I used to think, as a child, an angel sat
on my shoulder to watch over me. How I had related
that to the *Twilight Zone* episode with the evil
little leprechaun on the plane's wing. Every detail
should be used if it takes you someplace interesting.
For example, I often chew gum as I write. The man
most responsible for chewing gum is Generalissimo
Santa Anna, the villain of the Alamo, who moved
to Staten Island in the 1860s and took with him
some Mexican chicle, the dried sap of the sapodilla tree.
Chewing gum will stop your ears from popping during descent.
Thomas Adams invented sassafras gum, and his best
brand, "Black Jack," is the oldest on the market today.
In 1932, Nikola Tesla, inventor of alternating current
systems, declared that chewing exhausts
the salivary glands and leads to early death.
So now we have related several things: airplanes,
gum, TV science fiction shows, mythology, economics,
etymology, writing, history, science. In a few minutes
we will be at thirty-three thousand feet and can walk freely around
the cabin. We'll include a little biography and a reference to Italian
poetry, which is almost as unfashionable as mentioning painting.
This is something we both enjoy. However, I have rarely
seen you chew gum. In the event of a sudden loss in cabin
pressure, oxygen masks will drop from the compartment
above you. Your seat is also a flotation device.
Fifty-seven percent of Americans have dreamt of dying

in a plane crash. If only we knew how and when, we could
plan our lives more logically. The great logical rationalist,
Sir Isaac Newton (1642–1727) died from a nervous breakdown
brought on by mercury poisoning. He always feared
his passionate mysticism would be what drove him mad.
Franz Schubert's mental breakdown resulted from his syphilis
but this didn't stop him from writing his great symphony.
Since we are on this biographical digression—I must
tell you I hate any sort of digression that does not
transport us back to our original flight path, which is
my way of asking for your patience—take the case of
Torquato Tasso (1544–1595). His *Jerusalem Delivered*
is one of the great medieval epics, but he wandered mad
through Italy trying to forget everything he wrote.
When Byron visited his cell in Ferrara he wept.
In the end, Tasso lived in a kind of stable or cave
he painted with scenes from his poems to which he gave
a kind of comic twist as if to mock or ease his own
desperate pain. He had already forgotten how to say
he loved the world. He wanted to become an angel.
I can't help including all these details—it's like going
to a one-cent sale at the local mall. Maybe it's my fear
of losing anything, of losing you. In 1942 my uncle Bernard
flew his B-17 Flying Fortress into a Belgian woods,
letting the crew bail out. He wrote to my father a week before
about a secret he wanted to tell him but never did.
In the end, we are all going down. I nearly died in 1960
from blood poisoning. I wish I had been able to save
my father who ended up forgetting everyone. Consult the card
in the seat pocket in front of you for the location of all
emergency exits. Follow the instructions of the flight
attendants carefully. As if we could save anything. As if
we guarded the vaults of the moon. Tonight, the moon is
being eclipsed by our own planet. We are cutting out
its light. We never know what to say. We let Love mumble
a few words over coffee and walk out into the night.
We leave behind the shoes of our alibis. This is the time
to make your duty-free purchases. There are several specials.
You can almost see the angels outside your window.
The shadows of their wings have begun to ice over.
In a few minutes I'll actually begin the final draft

of this poem and you'll have gotten two for the price
of one. Meanwhile, we have already begun our descent.
This is the time you should try a little chewing gum.
The night has begun to abandon its wings.
Be careful in opening the overhead bins because details
may have shifted during flight. We are all on the red-eye
looking for home. Love is adjusting the flaps,
changing the angle of approach. No one expects it to last forever.
Keep your seat belts fastened until we come to a complete stop.
You seem to be carrying the morning on your shoulders.
What are you going to ask the moon as it floats away?

Things I Forgot to Put on My Reminder List

Turn off the coffee. Feed the cat. Lock the door.
Don't let the morning drift away like a barge.
Don't let sorrow drain the stars from the pond.
Don't try to colonize a lost past. Words like icebergs
breaking loose from the pack. The grammar of loss.
The heart being cannibalized. The mangrove of despair.
What else have I forgotten to pack? Everything
flares up in this fire like a pinecone dipped in wax.
The leg of the walking stick goes up like a match.
The light grabs everything like a hungry star.
How do we ever know what is important enough
to remember? History's promises knifing us in the back.
The snipers who have started to reload.
If only we could see them in those hills.
Why is it raining inside all the clocks?
The importance of remembering: of the nearly five
thousand heartbeats per hour, only one has to forget.
The shifting argument's of artillery positions.
The firelight falling, the embers forgetting the flame.
Those men in the Bosnian hills forced to bite off
each others' testicles. The souls carried there
in satchel charges. Hate dripping off the table
into the next century. What will be left for any of us?
Fix the screen, wash the car. Mow the lawn. To watch
the snail making its way up the side of a house
all night, leaving a history only we can understand.
Or the sky that lies shattered at your feet. To
peek through the keyhole of fate. To see how
the night still lingers in your eyes. The way my soul
levitates around you. The smell of overripe
peaches on the counter. How you open your eyes to me
in the morning. Maybe I should just crumple this list
into the fire. Maybe our hopes can no longer fly
like those two wild turkeys we saw yesterday.
Apples, coffee, juice. Is there any part of you
my mouth has not touched? My old self hanging
like a moth-eaten coat in a closet. Call the florist.
Mail the letters. Pick up the tickets. Check the maps.

Don't worry that the earth's inner core spins faster
and laps us every four hundred years. We are still here.
In spite of. In what way. In the meantime.
The wasps chasing us, getting caught in your hair.
The assassin's nightscope needing adjustments.
Time: the black ants eating the tree from the inside
out, always anticipating, always dreading
the moment they see light. Where would we live?
Don't worry, the heart always floats to the surface.
The essence of string theory in physics being
that we are all tied together by invisible emotions.
These words at your door like a nervous delivery
boy. Everything wants to take flight. The sparks
of this fire disappearing into the dark. The names
of the victims always written out of the treaty.
Where can we go with our squeaky fan belt,
our retread tires, our out-of-date maps?
Inside you, all roads unravel. Even before I touch you:
how you start to imitate the way the ground fog
wavers across the grass. Some nights the dew
seems to soak the stars. Your laugh settling
in the corners. Your words weeding the flowers.
The old doubts finally washing up on shore.
Paint the house. Trim the bushes. Patch the roof.
Get rid of the garbage. Return the calls. Turn off the lights.
Bandage the heart. Bandage the hour. Hold you
against the sky, against the future.
Each of us shadowboxing with eternity.
To let your voice halt the moon in its tracks.
To lean out over the balcony of desire.

The
Juniper
Prize

This volume is the twenty-fifth
recipient of the Juniper Prize
presented annually by the
University of Massachusetts Press
for a volume of original poetry.
The prize is named in honor of
Robert Francis (1901–1987), who lived
for many years at Fort Juniper,
Amherst, Massachusetts.

About the Author

Richard Jackson is the author of four previous books of poems—*Alive All Day* (1992), winner of the Cleveland State University Press Award, *Worlds Apart* (Alabama, 1989), *Part of the Story* (Grove, 1983) and *Heart's Bridge: Poems Based on Petrarch* (University of Toledo: Aureole, 1999). He is also the author of two chapbooks of imitations, one from Petrarch (*The Half Life of Dreams*) and one from six Renaissance Italian poets (*Love's Veils*), and a chapbook of Pavese's last poems, *The Woman in the Land,* all from Black Dirt Press in Elgin, Illinois. His two books of criticism are *Dismantling Time in Contemporary American Poetry,* winner of the Agee Prize, and *Acts of Mind: Interviews with Contemporary Poets.* Jackson edited *Double Vision: Four Slovene Poets* and a bilingual anthology of contemporary Slovene poetry, *The Fire Beneath the Moon.* A winner of NEA, NEH, Witter Bynner, *Crazyhorse* magazine, and other awards, he has been a Fulbright exchange poet to Yugoslavia and has won four Pushcart appearances. Jackson's poems have appeared in journals such as *North American Review, Crazyhorse, New England Review, Prairie Schooner, Georgia Review, Atlanta Review, Kenyon Review, Gettysburg Review, Antioch Review,* and *Harvard Review,* as well as journals in Romania, Slovenia, Serbia, Croatia, Italy, Poland, Hungary, Israel, Czech Republic, Spain, and Austria. A *Selected Poems* in Slovene and English will appear in Slovenia. Jackson teaches at the University of Tennessee at Chattanooga, where he has won several teaching awards, and he is on the staff of the Vermont College Masters of Fine Arts Program. He edits *Poetry Miscellany, Mala Revija: A Journal of Slovene Culture*, and the PM East European Chapbook series.